Anonymous

Silent Love

A Poem. Fourth English Edition

Anonymous

Silent Love
A Poem. Fourth English Edition

ISBN/EAN: 9783337401481

Printed in Europe, USA, Canada, Australia, Japan

Cover: Foto ©Andreas Hilbeck / pixelio.de

More available books at **www.hansebooks.com**

SILENT LOVE.

SILENT LOVE.

A POEM.

FIRST AMERICAN
FROM THE
FOURTH ENGLISH EDITION.

———

PHILADELPHIA:
ROBERT H. BALL.
1877.

SILENT LOVE.

O man e'er loved like me.   When but a boy
Love was my solace and my only joy;
Its mystic influence fired my tender soul,
And held me captive in its soft control !
By night it ruled in bright ethereal dreams,
By day in latent, ever-varying themes,—
In solitude, or 'mid the city's throng,
Or in the festal halls of mirth and song,—
Through loss or gain, through quietude or strife,
This was the charm, the heart-pulse of my life.

While age has not subdued the flame divine,

A votary still I worship at the shrine!

When cares enthral, or when the soul is free,

'Tis all the same. No man e'er loved like me!

O! SHE was young who won my yielding heart;

Nor power of poesy, nor the painter's art,

Could half the beauties of her mind portray,

E'en when inspired, and how can this my lay?

Two eyes that spoke what language ne'er can do,

Soft as twin-violets moist with early dew!

And on her cheeks the lily and the rose

Blent beauteously in halcyon repose;

While vermil lips, apart, reveal'd within

Two rows of pearls, and on her dimpled chin

The Graces smiled; a bosom heaved below

Warm as the sun, but pure as forest snow;—

Her copious ringlets hung in silken trains

O'er alabaster streak'd with purpling veins ;—

Her pencill'd eyebrows arching fair and high

O'er lids so pure they scarcely screen'd the eye!

A form symmetral, moving forth in grace

Like heaven-made Eve, the mother of our race ;

And on her brow benevolence and truth

Were chastely throned in meek, perennial youth,

While every thought that had creation there,

But made her face still more divinely fair,

And every fancy of her soul express'd

On that fair margin what inspired her breast,

Pure as the sunbeams gild the placid deep,

When zephyrs close their wings in listless sleep.

Thus maiden won my heart; O! is it vain

To say, perhaps hers was return'd again !—

To say, she read the language of my eyes,

And knew my thoughts unmingled with disguise!

Is it too much to say that eyes reveal

What words in vain but struggle to conceal,—

That SILENT love is not far more sincere

Than vaunting vows—those harbingers of fear!

Deep-rooted veneration breathes no sound ; —

Back, mortals, back, ye stand on holy ground!

Hid in the heart's recess, like precious ore,

It lies in brilliant beauty at the core!

Or, as the moon, sweet empress of the night!

Reflecting gives in modest mellowy light

The sun's refracting rays—her destined part—

So genuine feeling steals from heart to heart!

Laugh not, ye sordid sons, ye beings cold,

Who measure all your greatness by your gold,—

Whose marble bosoms never once could feel

What friendship, love, and sympathy reveal;

Learn but one truth, 'twill not reduce your stores,

Love higher than your gilded riches soars,

Your demi-god a meaner thing must be

Than Cupid proves.   No man e'er loved like me!

    THINK not a glance too transient to destroy

The calmness of the mind with mingled joy,—.

Judge for yourselves, but make no strictures here,

Set no mean limits to its hope and fear.

Many could tell, if they but had the art,

The stirring power with which it throbs the heart;

Thrills every nerve, pursues through every vein

Its path electric till it fires the brain,—

And trembling there like needle to the pole,

Strange blushes rise in crimson from the soul;

A*

The heaving breast in respiration free,

Convulsive feels with innate ecstasy.

But, then, that glance was quickly stolen away,

Love needs nor books, nor orator's display!

Fleet as the meteor's flight across the sky,

Is beauty's bright and love-revealing eye;

But, as it passes, like the meteor too,

Can kindle thoughts which time may ne'er subdue;—

Can raise a living passion in the soul,

A sage's prudence never could control—

Arouse the dormant senses of the heart,

And make it feel acute in every part—

Give softer language to the aqueous eye,

And make it roll in silence on the sky,

Till the expanding soul's refining thought

A marvellous sensibility has caught—

So keen, so calm, so tender, and so kind,

That earthly cares are scattered to the wind!

So each fond look was fraught with feverish pain,

That but renew'd the deathless hope again!

Creating sweetest charms and raptures gay,

That stole the stillness of my soul away!

Then came deep nights of doubt and darkness on,

When man is left contemplative alone;—

When fond philosophy usurps her reign,

Striving to have her sovereign sway again.

But all is nought when love pervades the breast,

What can reduce the feelings down to rest!

The dimpled god will still direct each dart,

With all his archful meaning, at the heart,—

Laughs when he sees you strive to thwart his aim,

And stirs anew the embers of the flame;

Retires, returns with face of lively joy,

And still delights in transports to annoy.

Riches and power, ye have no golden art,

Where shines the lighted censer of the heart!

Fame and its passions hurriedly decay,

For all is love, and love will have his way!

But, oh! when fate's stern mandates disapprove,

Then keenest are the burning darts of love,

The heart that's bound, then struggles to be free,

A pensive bird in sweet captivity.

Sick, sick at heart, o'ercome with doubt and woe,

My tears would gush like urns that overflow;

Aloud have I chastised my cherish'd fear,

And deem'd my love lack'd power to be sincere!

So does the timid fawn, on yonder hill,

In love and leisure wander at his will,

Till gazing on the lordly face of men,

He starts and springs in terror to his den ;

For love's a coward, even a very slave,

While boldness often fires the basest knave ;

And sadness, tears, and sickness could but be

Its inward strength, my soul's perplexity.

Thus did I feel and murmur when alone,

And said, this world's cold heart is hard as stone ;

'Twas error this, methinks I hear you say,

For there are hearts whose kindness ne'er decay !

That I was misanthropic so to feel,

And but my heart, no other heart was steel.

I know the world—have suffer'd too, its scorn,

And many treacherous calumnies have borne ;

Borne them in silence—to refute the same,

Had added new insult upon my name ;—

Seen the malicious smile, and envy too,

Strive all my dearest actions to undo,

And though inspired to do them aught but wrong,

Have known them sneer in malice on my song.

Why all this spleen—whence all this vain desire?

To strew the path with thorns where we aspire;

Striving to teach the world, with none avail,

The poet's strain a mere fictitious tale.

Vain thought! he dips his pencil in the light

Of rainbow tints, that suit his muse's flight;

Explores the hid recesses of the heart,

And feels in truth the essence of his art!

'Tis dread of overreaching them in thought,

Scarce worth the having, 'tis so dearly bought!

And this is man, to load with low disdain

A life of labour, mingled else with pain;

Then frown not, world, though wiser far ye be,

And colder too.   No man e'er loved like me!

Oft on the peopled streets, where mingled din

Disturbs the mind, whose thoughts are turn'd within,

In haste emerging from the moving throngs,

Where every face portrays its inward wrongs !

We two have met, then through my troubled heart

The sudden glance has pierced me like a dart ;

My frame grown paralyzed, my eyes cast down,

As when a child receives a father's frown.

Ah ! then, for hours I've struggled in dismay,

Unfit to follow on her hallow'd way,

To watch her steps, perchance to hear her voice,

Which would have made my very soul rejoice ;

Then all, unnoticed, friend or foe, pass'd by

Without the recognition of mine eye ;

The world, and all its inharmonious sound,

Silenced and seal'd in musings most profound,

Till startled into life, roused from the theme,

I would awake like sluggard from a dream,

And gazing round in stupor and surprise,

First on the earth and then upon the skies—

Myself I would upbraid most piteously,

And still exclaim—No man e'er loved like me!

WHAT fann'd the flame and made it brighter glow?

A power within, which Stoics never know!

Perchance we often met—I say not where,—

But where, alas! no words, but glances were.

And then electric magic from each glance

Stole through my bosom like a burning lance;—

Spoke to my spirit with a spirit's voice,

And made my soul in ecstasy rejoice!

A soft benignity of look was there,

A gleam of joy, a shadow of despair,

As fleecy clouds that glide o'er Luna's face,

But scarcely dim a portion of her grace,

Peopling my brain with new created themes,

That only lover knows, or poet dreams ;—

Pour'd noontide beams of glory o'er my soul

In light ethereal with divine control,

And hopes too high, too holy e'er to be

Enjoy'd, o'ercame me with sublimity !

I KNEW her home, and often pass'd that way,

Sure as the sun perform'd his course each day ;

Then at her lattice, beaming like the morn,

I saw the maid that made my heart forlorn ;

Though by this heavenly hope the spell was rear'd,

Our mutual prudence declaration fear'd ;

Yet could I mark her straining, longing eyes,

Beam like twin stars through partly-shrouded skies.

Scoff not—for years I still pursued this art,

In hopes to wile the angel to my heart;

In hopes to meet, to breathe the latent spell,

And if unkind, to sigh and say farewell !

Such things, I said, have been, and still may be,

One only holds futurity's gold key.

O ! IF the gods live on ambrosial food,

By mortals named, nor seen, nor understood—

So hope unseen by any eyes save mine,

Fed my young heart with nutriment divine !

Rear'd me to feel with glowing soul of joy

The charms of love, though otherwise a boy.

The cup was sweet, I drank its deepest drop,

And still relied on never-dying hope.—

O Hope! thou sweet deceiver of the world!

Thy banner is too temptingly unfurl'd—

How many seek thy phantom form to trace,

Till sorrow clouds the sunshine of the face!

Led on and on by thy delusive sway,

Till youth and beauty languish both away,—

Till undeceived, we murmur, but in vain—

For who can turn to youth's gay morn again!

Ah me! if I should own thy sov'reign power,

Who dares to blame? See buds in every bower.

Whose lives are like to man's, a fleeting day—

Nursed up in hope to blossom and decay!

Rear'd by the dewy smiles of laughing morn,

Behold the rose adorn its native thorn,—

At mid-day throwing forth its rich perfume,—

At evening bending sadly o'er its tomb,

Yet in its death a fragrance leaves behind,

Like retrospective thoughts within the mind!

Methinks I see some aged cynic smile,

And say, thou art the dupe of thine own guile—

Your actions could no better end declare,

For foolishness must always bring despair!

Pshaw! simpletons, your greatest wisdom lies

In the mean leer that lurks about your eyes,—

In the deceitful grin that clothes your cheek,

In the slow accents of your language sleek;

Your life is spurn'd, and so your pedigree,

And self-esteem.   No man e'er loved like me!

She was a child when first our glances met,

Now womanhood upon her brow had set;

Still look'd she lovely, lovelier than before!

A creature every eye might well adore,

At least I thought so—love may have the power

To make the meanest weed appear a flower,—

Look through a medium always soft and kind,

Like distant landscapes pictured on the mind!

Love gazes through a focus of its own,

To other eyes unseen and all unknown;

So, if she still was lovely to my eye,

What should I care though all her charms decry,

I scarcely wish'd that other eyes should see

Her chasten'd worth, for she was all to me!

O SACRED Love! how innocent art thou!

No malice sits on thy devoted brow—

No discord jars the strings around thy heart;

Thou art an heavenly feeling, every part!

No earthly lusts pollute thy chasten'd name,

These are consumed to embers in the flame!

In all the strange arcana of the mind,

Nought but their merest dust is left behind.

A brighter and more glorious spirit reigns—

A livelier current circles through the veins,

New thoughts, new fancies, hopes, and chaste desire,

With varied joys, that never, never tire!

Sweet inspiration, with its wondrous charm,

Like power magnetic, draws the soul from harm;

Yet, ever mingled with incessant fear,

Our joys partake the moisture of a tear;

Since first of time it has been so, 'twill be

While life holds on, its marvellous mystery.

So, thus inspired, I chose her as my muse,

No better goddess could my bosom choose!

The heathens had their deities, but she

Was less obscure, and more divine to me:

But still in song I never breathed her name,

Fearful my feeble verse might cause her shame—

Fearful that such a liberty might chase

The partial smile of favour from her face.

Fearful the sneering world too might know

The favourite maid, who caused my latent woe,

And by the idle mouth of rumour quell

The fervid spirit of a cherish'd spell.

No confidant had I, such I disown!

Mine was a secret never to be known.

Nature had thrown her fairest robes away,

To weep in sackcloth on that fatal day!

Deep in my breast I treasured and revered

That holy word, and there its tendrils rear'd;

It never, never shall in utterance be

A vulgar sound.   No man e'er loved like me!

What's in a name? "A rose would smell as sweet

By any other," is a trite conceit!

Names give abhorrence if they are unkind,

A pain, a leprous feeling to the mind!

Names that are wed to deeds of base desire,

Set holy feelings in the breast on fire;

Association lingers in the sound,

The sore long cured becomes a second wound;

Sad retrospection wakens up anew

Perhaps the pains of one who was untrue,

Where kind oblivion had her olive hung

In gentle peace to ease a bosom wrung.

There is a secret something that controls

With spectral gloom our never-slumbering souls;

We look aghast, and struggle to conceal

The shock, that might a thousand truths reveal,

And, as the recollection fades away,

So sunbeams fall upon our dark dismay;

The branchy streams of life, a moment still,

Resume their course and mitigate the ill.

"What's in a name?" I can too plainly tell!

A wondrous, inward-working, sacred spell,

That wheresoe'er one name escaped man's lips,

My spirit rose from out its dark eclipse,

And in the Sacred book I often found

The impress dear with heavenly halo bound!

And angel forms seem'd whispering in mine ear

The accents of the name I loved so dear.

O! when I met with one who own'd the same,

My heart's pulsations quicker went and came;

All other thoughts were banish'd by the sound;

My filming eyes fix'd thoughtful on the ground;

Silence has bound my tongue and chain'd my feet,

Struck by the accents of a sound so sweet,

And those around have whisper'd in mine ear—

Wherefore arises that instinctive tear?

Wherefore? Ah! let none save an angel speak

In strains celestial and serenely sweet!

An heavenly feeling fill'd my conscious heart,

Like fancied music which the spheres impart;

No earth-taught tongue could in its might disclose

The eloquence it pour'd upon my woes;

Even heard from children in their wanton glee,

'Twas youth-renewing ecstasy to me.

WHAT time I went to rest, what time I rose,

My mind was throng'd with all these joys and woes,

'Mid sunlit scenes, in sylvan beauty green,

When morning minstrels sung the leaves between;

Methought I heard them chant in rapturous tone,

Get wed! get wed! why languish thus alone?

Or when the glorious sun roll'd down the west,

And clouds lay lambent in their golden rest;

Or when cool evening wept her dew on flowers,

To quench their thirst and spangle dædal bowers,

There was no change—the pure ethereal theme

Felt no exhausted fondness in its dream,

But reign'd and ruled an empress glad and free,

With boundless sway, in endless monarchy.

'Twas absence, like a spell, that chiefly bound

My captive heart with firmer irons round.

Absence, thou cheat of sight, thou more than blind

And dark deceiver! wherefore so unkind,

To hide that heaven on earth I long'd to see?

O sightless eyes! No man e'er loved like me!

Through shadowy glade, or by meandering rill,

Where all but Nature's eloquence is still,

I, in the depth of uncontroll'd despair,

Address my sorrow to the soft-ear'd air.

O loved one of my bosom! gentlest maid!

Say, have I e'er thy tender truth betray'd?

Does pensive silence wound thy heart like mine,

Or has oblivion seal'd the charm divine?

Have Lethe's waters, pouring o'er thy mind,

Sunk all the varying passions, once so kind?

Or was I wrong to look for love return'd,

Though wildly and sincere this bosom burn'd?

Alas! what reasons ever can explain

Such soul-consuming and unspoken pain?

A mutual mingling of two sprites above

Can only give a semblance of my love!

O WOMAN! woman! ever true and kind,

Thou sweet perfection of the gentle mind!

Blest to refine thy lord-like brother-man,

The last, but noblest of the Almighty's plan!

How calm, how tender, and how full of love,

An earthly angel sent him from above;—

A being in whose soft expressive eyes

We read the light, the language of the skies!

WHAT time the dulcet accents of thy voice

Mine ear receives, they make my heart rejoice;

What time I see thy graceful form divine,

I feel in truth that loveliness is thine;—

And in thy smile what matchless beauties blend,

Thou chasten'd gift! thou everlasting friend!

TEACH me, ye muses! to portray her praise

In words of living fire, that burn always;

Let me unfold, in every glowing line,

Some charm, O woman! that alone is thine;

Inspire my pen, and dip it in my heart,

Let not a thought be chill'd by rigid art;

Chain to remembrance all my bosom feels;

Let time move slower on its viewless wheels,

Till all is writ on adamant, to stand

So long as light illumes my native land!

O MAINSPRING of domestic love and joy!

Can man have haunts that would thy peace destroy?

Can any pleasures which these scenes impart

Float with such genuine feeling round the heart?

Can gay companionship, or false desire,

More than their moment, mortal breasts inspire?

Ah! no—in such society as thine,

Man only knows where truth and duty shine!

To thee alone belongs the siren power

To keep the odour in life's fading flower;

To thee alone belongs the power to bind

The vernal growth of glory to the mind,

And man, however great and good he be,

Soon turns a blank, if once he turns from thee!

WITH what ensanguine words shall I impart

The genuine love that fills the mother's heart;

That fond delight which glows in rapturous joy—

Nor poverty nor sickness can destroy,

When the first artless smile of love is given,

Which makes her baby more a thing of heaven,

And on the dimpling cheek of peachy hue

This sign of recognition meets her view.

WHEN cares, like age, creep o'er us and destroy

The transitory flush of hope and joy,

Her glowing tear of sympathy outvies

The spangly dew that on the violet lies,

Distilling purely from affection's well,

Where all the pearls of dear attraction dwell.

O blissful thought! to see thee smile through these,

And all to give the burthen'd bosom ease ;—

O more than sainted sight, far more than earth,

When we reflect the feeling's genuine birth—

To soften man, to lead him from his care ;—

To wash away the stains of dark despair ;—

To reconcile his bosom to his fate,

O this is surely, truly, being great!

Is thy heart gay, what can with thee compare?

What votive transports make thee still more fair?

Can the vermilion add a sweeter hue,

Or art excel where all is purely true?

Can wealth or earthly vanities inspire,

Where love has set the vestal heart on fire?

Careless alike of their too mean control,

Heaven holds a higher banquet in the soul!

And Nature, as at first, free, undefiled,

Makes thee again as sinless as a child!

Does man desert thee, turn and love no more;

Is thy soft passion then as fleetly o'er?—

Ah, no! Is there in yonder varied bower

A fragile plant, a winter-breathing flower,

That, by degrees, droops into pale decay,

And wanes in silent loneliness away?

E'en so fade hopes and happiness in thee—

Emblem of spring—heir of eternity!

She was the heroine, then, of every tale

That flush'd my cheek, or made it sickly pale;

B*

In dreams I saw her vision'd forth in joy,

And felt as young and buoyant as a boy!

Heard her discourse of future joys, and tell

How much she loved, and thought she loved too well;

Thus fancy ever form'd ideal things,

Till I could hear the rustling of the wings

Of beings of the sky.—To love is given

A power to feel and taste the joys of heaven!

Hear with new ears, to see with seer-like eyes,

And, phœnix-like, from fear's pale ashes rise!

WHEN love was young, the gods celestial lay

On gold-tinged clouds that hemm'd the skirts of day;

Gazing in glory from their couch on high,

A misty globe seem'd rolling down the sky,

And on its disc two speck-like forms did move—

The earliest pair wed to devoted love;

'Twas Eve and Adam wandering hand in hand,

The sole possessors of that sphere-like land!

Inspiring love! who shall thy powers portray,

Howe'er unbless'd thy votaries fade away?

Bridle the winds, set limits to the sea,

Bid wandering clouds to be no longer free;

Call eagles from the air on high, and bid

The hills decay, and in the seas be hid;

Tell Spring it must not bud, and Autumn brown

To keep its leaves and throw no foliage down;

Bid structures rise in rows at thy command,

Without materials or the artist's hand;

Teach man to live on air, and rocks to fly,

Tell birds no more to roam the ambient sky:

Do all these things,—when ye so powerful prove,

Then put your definitions upon love.

Love framed the world, and love created man,

Love is the soul of the infinite plan;

Love is the spring of every glorious deed,

Love makes the patriot for his country bleed;

Love is the bliss of every Christian mind,

Love makes the generous to the needful kind;

Love makes the mother o'er her infant weep,

When death has closed its eyes in icy sleep;

Love bids the heathen worship at the sun,

Where truth and science have not yet begun;

Love made famed Wallace like a lion bold,

When she he loved was basely slain of old;

Love was the parent of the tear first shed,

When gentle Eve beheld her Abel dead;

Love breathes more sweet than seraph ever sung,

Its accents are too soft for human tongue;

Love has its sighs, on whose fair wings is borne

A beam of gladness brighter than the morn;

Love makes me write this retrospective lay,

Whatever readers think, or critics say!

Hush, then, nor deem it wisdom to be free

Of love's gold links.—No man e'er loved like me!

O! WHEREFORE then in anguish pine away?

Thus oft mine inward monitor would say;

Why not declare, in words not yet express'd,

The secret, silent sorrow of thy breast?

It shall be so, I boldly would reply,

And then reviving gladness lit mine eye;

It shall be so. O vain! O weak desire!

Dissolving like the snow when cast on fire.

Alas! alas! even when I grasp'd the pen,

I felt I could not act like other men—

3

A tremulous feeling shook my very frame,

I could not breathe, I could not write her name.

O sad resolve! how quickly wouldst thou fly

Upon the pinions of a pensive sigh!

For prudence, when it rules the mind aright,

With hope and doubt—alternate day and night—

Creates a fearful feeling, half insane!

Which dreads the merest semblance of disdain;

This wondrous sensibility of mind

Can brook no look, no accent that's unkind;

A *no*, instead of *yes*,—no more! no more!

The very thought sends poison to the core;

For this might to the sanguine soul convey

A dreaded fate, a desperate dismay,

An humbled, an abash'd and startling pain,

That might no more be curb'd by reason's rein.

Better, O better far! in each degree,

Unspoken wish.—No man e'er loved like me!

Thus oft I long'd to tell my secret mind

To some dear friend whose sympathies were kind,

That we might meet, as if it were by chance,

Round festive board, or in the mazy dance;

But, oh! I durst not speak the tremulous tale,

So often sigh'd on evening's dewy gale,—

So deeply graven on each page of life,

The source of all my happiness and strife;

Yet when I oped the guest-inclosing door,

And tript in lightness o'er the velvet floor,

I've gazed around with wild and wond'ring stare,

Perhaps to see if such an one were there;

Ah! then my anxious spirit would grow still,

And reason reign with more quiescent will,

For what I long'd so much in joy to greet,

My timid spirit could not brook to meet.

I could not trust my heart, full well I knew

A sudden glance would all my frame subdue;—

Would thus expose the workings of my soul,

O'er which my manhood could not hold control.

She never came—O strange, O weak dismay !

Thus, day and night, my hours stole sad away,

For ever bent on one engrossing theme,

Yet all uncertain as a poet's dream !

At last I left my home, went far away

To mix with crowds of strangers, where the gay

And gorgeous wheels of luxury roll along

In an outvying and tumultuous throng !

Where painted pride and mimicry conspire

To peep contemptuous from their gay attire,

And toys in artificial, fond display,

Sleep all the morn to gild the eve of day!

Lolling in soft and indolent repose,

As if the poor lack'd none to soothe their woes.

O! HEARTS diseased by pride and fashion's glow,

Are these the only raptures that ye know?

Is there no joy in cheering lonely hearts,—

In plucking from fell poverty its darts?

Is there no aged breast by want subdued?

No flowers to spread where thorns are only strew'd?

No sympathy, no gentle hand to give

To woe-worn wretches who scarce care to live?

Your pleasures cannot charm my marvelling eye,

Go teach those ones to smile whose life's a sigh;—

Go ease the couch of death—of deep dismay,—

'Twill give relief when earthly joys decay.

I've sought your haunts to mitigate my care,

But, ah! ye but contrast a world's despair;

So hapless beings fly to banish woe,

Forgetting 'tis within where'er they go.

Earth's noblest sights, earth's wonder-working men,

Cannot obliterate my immortal ken!—

The smile of peer or princess has no power

To wile my loved one from my breast an hour;

In every changeful scene, O! only she

Is present most, and holds supremacy.

Long, long, I wander'd 'mid the gay and fair,

Striving to seem the happiest mortal there;—

Striving to soothe my sad, my chequer'd life,

And thus extract sweet comfort from my strife.

Alas! they knew not, when they saw me smile,

Another charmer charm'd me all the while.

I wore her beauteous image in my soul;

Through every thought the dear enchantment stole!

Through every vein I felt her being move,

Inhaled her spirit and exhaled her love!

The dreamy cup I drank of sparkling hope,

And suck'd it still, to drain the latest drop;

Deep in my breast, like dew-drop in a flower,

It lay conceal'd, but gave refreshing power;

Till high enraptured with the draught divine,

My soul dissolved at the enhallow'd shrine!

Though poor the world, yet in one person join'd,

Beauty and wealth more often meet than mind!

But she was mind to me, an endless theme

That fed my day-thoughts and my midnight dream;

The joy of life, from which I always drew

Something delicious, something ever new!

Yet absence oft brought sorrow o'er my mind,

Like dark clouds sailing on the summer wind,

Till lost in thought, subdued in heart and speech,

Unbroken silence countless fears would teach;

And then they said, he treads his native hills,

And gazes fondly on their foaming rills,—

Sees the proud eagle in its heavenward flight

Towering above, 'mid clouds of storm and night!—

When dark-soul'd winter o'er his cottage hung,

And feeling, hope, and life itself were young!

Hears downward streams, that, as they glide along,

Have all their own and most peculiar song;—

Draws beauty from the lakes, health from the breeze

That sails the surface of the weltering seas—

Nor love, nor art, nor sorrow could they see

In all my acts.—No man e'er loved like me!

THINK of a bosom wrung with deep despair,

Between sweet hope, sad doubt, and joy and care;

Say what you will, or what you would have done,

Ye speak the words of folly every one!

Say, then, could I, whose boyhood grew in love,

Throw off its chains, and all its charms disprove?

As well might eagle caged, with starry eye,

Assume to rise in gladness to the sky;

As well might captive in his dungeon-cell

Take ease by purling brook or heathery dell,

Or mother, weeping o'er her only child

That death had chill'd, be from her grief beguiled,

And slaves console themselves that they are free

While irons clank.—No man e'er loved like me!

YET deem me not in fancy weak or vain

In echoing forth this sad pathetic strain;

'Tis but to prove what love can still deny,

When wealth and influence would affection buy!

'Tis but to show the sceptic he is wrong

In saying love cannot endure so long;

Exclaiming—all is madness—as his soul

Has never known its magical control.

Think for yourselves—but like a culprit I

Was doom'd for her to live, for her to die!

She bound my spirit with magnetic chains,

One hour of bliss was mine for years of pains!

Yet all these pains were mingled with a charm

That could the world's cold, selfish arts disarm,

Engendering new ideas as they swept

The pensile clouds where love dominion kept,

And, passing through Hope's crucible, refined

The ruder thoughts that rule the common mind;

I would not lose the joy for all the pain,

Though doom'd to tread the rugged path again!

Still could I cherish buds that bleakly grew,

Cast forth their seeds and watch their growth anew,

For I had given my heart with vows most true,

And if I'd had another, had given it too!

Yet in my grief I languish'd to be free,

So strange is thought—so weak humanity!

TIRED of a land of strange and selfish men,

I sought my Scottish mountain-home again,

And when I leap'd upon the rock-ribb'd strand,

Methought I felt the pressure of her hand—

Methought I saw her smile, and heard her say—

Welcome, O! welcome, wherefore did ye stray?

Speak as thou wilt, but with these hands I'll bind

Myself to thee, and know thy inmost mind!

O then I breathed the burden of my heart,

Nor longer seal'd my soul, while at each part

She hung her head and answer'd to my sighs

With tears of love depending from her eyes!

Methought I kiss'd her cheek.—O heaven! what joy,

After a winter of prolong'd alloy—

Methought I clasp'd her gently in my arms,

And in their folds embraced a world of charms!

I heard her voice, 'twas soft and silvery clear,

Like angel's accents steal upon mine ear,—

I gazed with transport in her face so fair,

And love's devotion reign'd in triumph there!

Anon her tears would flow with very joy,

And then my heart return'd them like a boy!

While utterance died a martyr in my breast,

And what I long'd to say was unexpress'd.

O soft delusive charm!   O vision'd joy!

Why is your triumph only to annoy?

Why is the path of love so wildly high,

With rocks and ramparts mingling with the sky?

Alas! the dream was short, the moment gay,

Vanish'd too soon in nothingness away;

For when I reach'd her home with anxious pain,

Determined thus my secret to explain,

She, she was gone, gone to her lasting rest,

The generous passion wither'd in her breast;

Gone with her maiden-grief, gone ne'er to be—

And yet I live.—O piteous destiny!

And yet I live to personate my woe,

A lingering shadow, moving to and fro!

Live still when all my earthly hopes are fled—

When all that gave enchantment now is dead!

Mark'd more by grief and solitary thought,

Than e'er on heart of hapless mortal wrought;—

Than ever thrill'd the plastic mind of man,

Whose secret might cold learning cannot scan;

Sad retrospection striving to destroy

The autumn of a life that else were joy;

Hope wither'd like a flower when winter chill

From arctic regions comes with direful will,

With all the rooted blessing of my mind

Torn up and strewn in handfuls on the wind!

Time's finger hath done much, my silvery hair

But partly shrouds a brow of lined despair!

But sorrow hath done more, hath sear'd my soul,

And writ this awful history on its scroll;

And when I leave this earth to soar on high,

O may her spirit meet me in the sky!

O may we then declare a mutual love,

If spirits blend in harmony above.

In firm reliance on this hope divine,

May calmer grief and holier thought be mine!

My tale is told, let all who read the same

Forgive its faults—I ask no better fame!—

Forgive the ardour of a love so strange,

That, 'mid all other changes, knew no change;

My heart is lighten'd by this honest lay,

And, for a time, has thrown its load away.

A leaden weight that but too sadly bore

A vital ulcer, eating to the core,

And in its path puissant stole along

The living chords that whilom thrill'd with song!

I've traced my love from childhood into age,

And mark'd its growth in every echoing page,

With soul-felt candour only as my aim,

Which ever lives through endless time the same!

O may your loves be happier far than mine!

Dread not to worship at the sainted shrine;

Let reason guide you, look for sweet success,

Nor sicken at the tale of my distress.

Seek truth, be faithful, worth is more than gold;—

Worth cheers the heart when other charms grow old!

With first love's joys, O may ye blessed be.

One truth believe—No man e'er loved like me!